This Golden Book belongs to

_____

_____

My Christmas Book of Numbers

Photos by Claudia Kunin

Special thanks to Alexander's Florist, Silver Lake, California,
for providing poinsettias and wreaths.

A GOLDEN BOOK · NEW YORK
Western Publishing Company, Inc., Racine, Wisconsin 53404
Packaged by the RGA Publishing Group, Inc.

1 one

There is only **one**
Santa Claus! He gives
presents to children
all over the world.

2 two

Santa has helpers called elves. How many elves do you see?
Yes, there are **two**!

3 three

We like to sing Christmas carols. How many carolers are we? One, two, **three!**

4 four

Here we play on our Christmas drums. Can you count **four** of them?

5 five

We are decorating **five** Christmas wreaths.

6 six

Here are **six** poinsettia plants. They are red and green— the colors of Christmas!

7 seven

How many Christmas stockings cover our toes?
The answer is **seven**!

8 eight

Eight reindeer! Santa's reindeer pull his sleigh on Christmas Eve.

9 nine

I made some Christmas cards. How many did I make? **Nine!**

10 ten

Christmas is a time of giving. This year I have **ten** presents to give to my family and friends.

12 twelve

Candy canes are a special Christmas treat—and I have **twelve**!

15 fifteen

We have Christmas bells to ring—**fifteen** in all!

20 twenty

Twenty candles are glowing. What a nice way to say "Merry Christmas!"